She made her bed so quickly that it was more of a mess afterward than when she started!

little Miss Quick

by Roger Hargreaves

PSS!
PRICE STERN SLOAN

Little Miss Quick was always in a terrible hurry and she was always trying to get everything done as quickly as she could.

Now, all this rushing around meant that Little Miss Quick was very careless.

When she brushed her teeth, she squeezed the toothpaste out of the tube so quickly that it went everywhere.

Everywhere, that is, except on her toothbrush.

One sunny autumn morning, Little Miss Quick got up even more quickly than usual, and made her bed and combed her hair in her quick and careless way.

After a breakfast of bread (Little Miss Quick was always in far too much of a hurry to wait for the toaster!), she ran out of her house like a whirlwind, and left the door open, as usual.

One minute later, and three miles from her house, Little Miss Quick came to a sudden stop.

The postman was standing in her way.

"You have far too many letters to deliver," she said. "Let me help you."

And she delivered the letters very quickly.

But also very carelessly!

The postman was very angry.

In fact, he was so angry that he chased after Little Miss Quick . . .

. . . but she was already miles away.

She had met Mr. Strong.

"That basket of eggs looks heavy," she said.
"Let me help you carry it back to your house."

And before Mr. Strong had had a chance to say
"no," or even blink for that matter, Little Miss
Quick had carried the eggs back to his house
very quickly . . .

. . . and, needless to say, very carelessly!

When he saw that all his eggs were broken, Mr. Strong was furious.

In fact, he was so furious that he also chased after Little Miss Quick.

But she was already miles away.

She was at the zoo, talking to the zookeeper.

"You must be tired of feeding all these lions.
Let me feed them for you," she said.

Then before you could say "Little Miss Quick," she
had picked up a bucket of corn and rushed off.

And she fed the lions in her usual quick . . . and
very careless way.

Lions hate corn!

But they love doors that are open.

So it happened that, on that sunny autumn morning, Little Miss Quick found herself surrounded by a very angry postman, a furious Mr. Strong, a terrified zookeeper, and two hungry lions.

What do you think she did?

That's right!

Quick as a shot she said to herself, "I'd better get out of here as quickly as ever I can and . . ."

". . . as carefully as possible!"